HAPPY EASTER

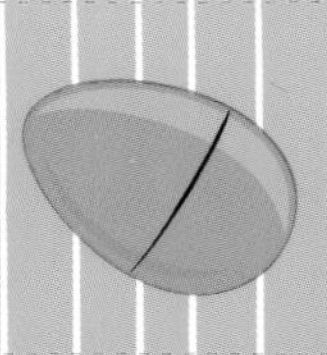

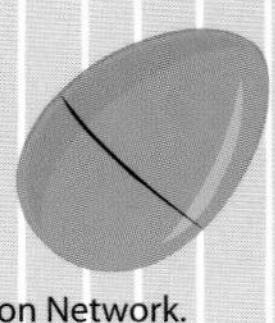
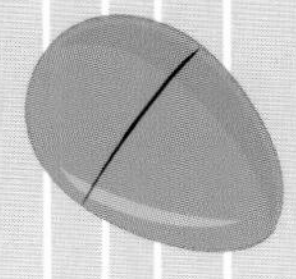

Punch out these egg stands and use them to support your Easter eggs!

C-RD9-89949-4

SIDEKICK SHOWDOWN

By Tracey West

Based on
FOSTER'S HOME FOR IMAGINARY FRIENDS,
as created by Craig McCracken

SCHOLASTIC INC.

New York Toronto London Auckland Sydney
Mexico City New Delhi Hong Kong Buenos Aires

ISBN-13: 978-0-439-89949-9
ISBN-10: 0-439-89949-4

12 11 10 9 8 7 6 5 4 3 2 1 7 8 9 10 11

Printed in the U.S.A.
First printing, February 2007

Designed by Kim Brown

The city was in chaos! A giant Imaginary Friend stomped through the streets.

"Don't panic!" Frankie yelled. "It's perfectly harmless!"

But the extremosaurus didn't seem to know that. It charged at Mac, its big mouth opened wide . . .

. . . when an imaginary superhero swooped down from the sky! He scooped up Mac and saved him from the beast.

Imaginary Man blasted the extremosaurus with his orange soda soaker. He pounded it with a giant paddleball. The city was saved!

Imaginary Man helped Frankie take the extremosaurus back to Foster's Home for Imaginary Friends.

"Imaginary Man, thank you for saving my life today. You're awesome!" Mac said.

"Awesome-rific!" the hero corrected Mac. "Want to take a ride in my awesome-rific supersonic sidecar?"

Bloo scowled. "We're supposed to be working on our tree house!"

The next day, Bloo and Mac went to the store to get supplies for their tree house. Suddenly, an Imaginary Friend with pink hair robbed the hardware store.

"That's Nemesis!" Mac cried. "Imaginary Man's archenemy!"

Mac contacted Imaginary Man on his communicator.

Mac and Imaginary Man found Nemesis downtown. She had prettied up the whole place with ribbons and scented candles!

"I will give the whole world a makeover and everything will be beautiful!" Nemesis laughed.

"You fiend!" Imaginary Man yelled.

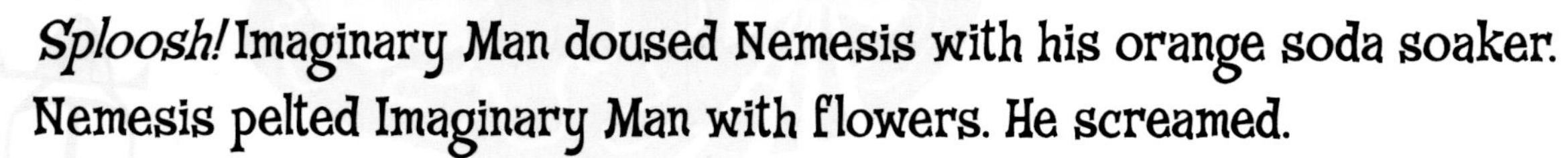

Sploosh! Imaginary Man doused Nemesis with his orange soda soaker.

Nemesis pelted Imaginary Man with flowers. He screamed.

"Flowers are Imaginary Man's kryptonite," said Mac, worried. "They're sucking away his powers!"

Mac jumped in front of Imaginary Man. He protected the hero from the flowers.

Imaginary Man was impressed. "Mac, will you be my sidekick?" he asked.

"Yes! Yes! I will be your sidekick!" Mac replied.

Bloo looked on in horror. He was losing his best friend to a sappy superhero!

The next day, Bloo was happy to see that the tree house was finished. Until he saw that Mac and Imaginary Man were using it as their headquarters!

"I figured out that Nemesis's hairdo is the source of all her powers," Mac said. "And I think I know where she's getting it fixed!"

"Good work, Mac-Attack!" Imaginary Man said.

Bloo sat down at the breakfast table, feeling sad. Then he got an idea.

"I know how to get Mac back!" he cried. He tied the tablecloth around his neck. "I'll become the greatest superhero the world has ever known!"

Mac and Imaginary Man sped to the Salon de Sissé. They found Nemesis getting her hair done.

Mac quickly destroyed all of the flowers in sight. Then Imaginary Man belched on Nemesis's hair. It looked like she was defeated for good, when . . .

"The Azure Avenger is here!" Bloo cried.

But Bloo's tablecloth cape still had all the breakfast stuff on it. A vase of flowers fell from his cape . . . and onto Imaginary Man's face.

"Aaargh! Petunias!" the hero screamed.

Nemesis got away again.

Mac and Imaginary Man left Bloo on the floor of the salon. Nemesis appeared behind him.

"You want revenge, don't you?" she asked. "Then join me!"

Hours later, in the dark of night, Bloo's transformation was complete. "Lord Uniscorn, rise!" Nemesis commanded.

The battle between Imaginary Man and Mac-Attack and Nemesis and Lord Uniscorn began.

Nemesis and Uniscorn replaced a football team's uniforms with prom dresses. They switched monster-truck fuel with perfume. They even gave a makeover to a rock band!

But no matter what they did, everyone cheered for Imaginary Man and Mac-Attack.

Lord Uniscorn was disgusted. "No more cute!" he screamed at Nemesis. "I will no longer accept the plans that you plan! From now on, we go forward with the plans that I plan, and the ones that I plan on planning!"

"Fine," Nemesis said. "So what's your stupid plan?"

The next day, Imaginary Man flew toward Mac's school. "Three o'clock. Time for the daily patrol!" he said cheerfully. But Mac was nowhere to be found! Imaginary Man zoomed toward Foster's Home . . . and saw the place was painted pink!

Imaginary Man found Mac in the laundry room tied to a chair.

"It's a trap!" Mac warned.

But he was too late. The laundry chute above them burst open. A mountain of flowers fell on Imaginary Man!

"No!" Mac cried.

Lord Uniscorn entered. “It is I who will be your best friend now that Imaginary Fool is gone forever!” the villain cackled.
“I will never be your best friend!” Mac yelled.
“But Mac, I am your father!” Lord Uniscorn said.
“What?” asked Mac.

"*Aaaargh!*" Lord Uniscorn fell to the floor as one of Nemesis's rainbow rays blasted him in the back. His mask fell off.

"Bloo?" Mac exclaimed.

"How dare you turn on me, Uniscorn!" Nemesis wailed. "I who created you! I who befriended you! Plus, I thought we had something special."

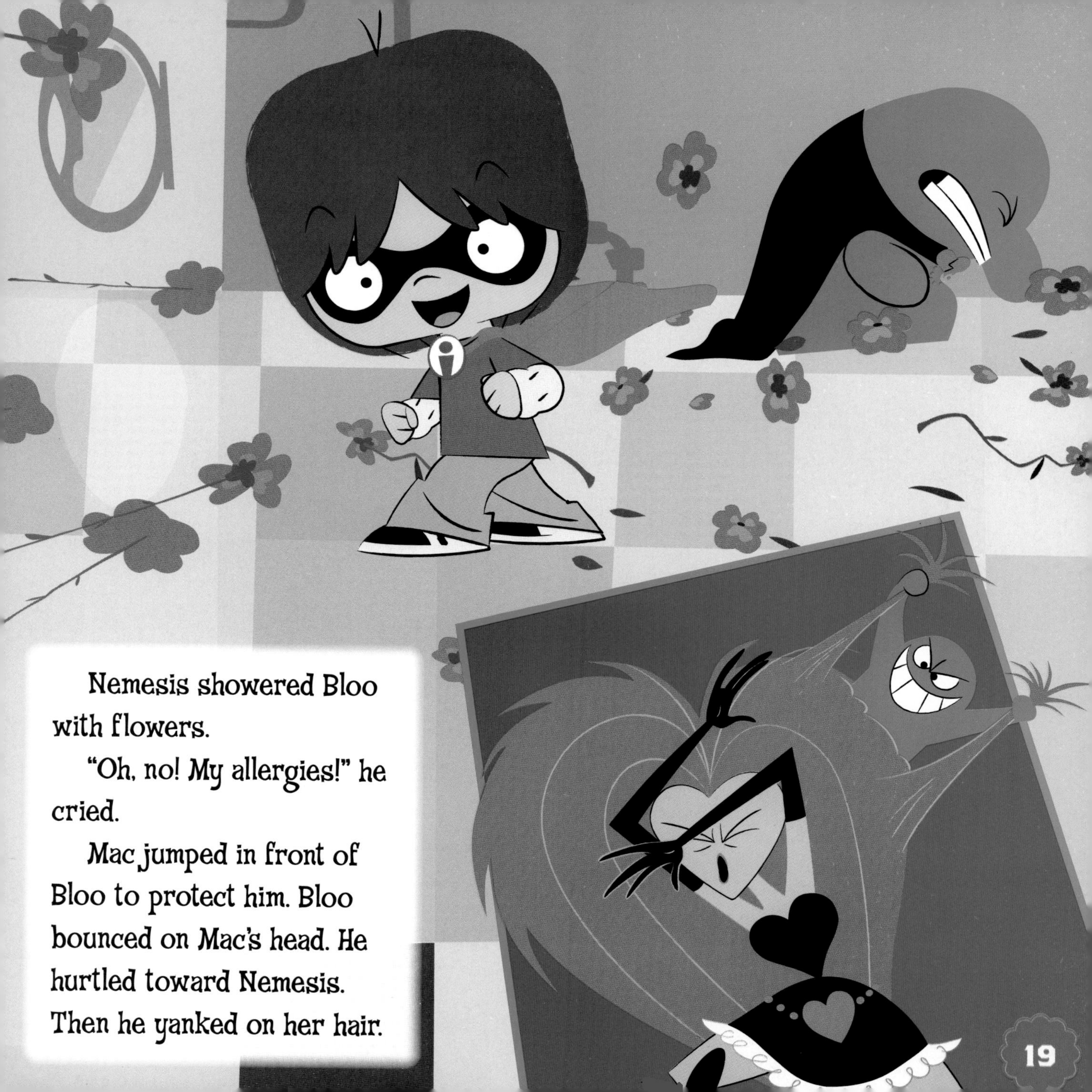

Nemesis showered Bloo with flowers.

"Oh, no! My allergies!" he cried.

Mac jumped in front of Bloo to protect him. Bloo bounced on Mac's head. He hurtled toward Nemesis. Then he yanked on her hair.

Imaginary Man pushed through the flowers.

"Nobody pulls my Neme-sister's hair but me!" he yelled.

Mac and Bloo looked at each other in shock. "Neme-sister?"

Mr. Herriman helped figure out the mystery. Years ago, a boy had imagined Imaginary Man. His sister had imagined Nemesis just to bug him.

The brother and sister were all grown up now, but they thought Imaginary Man and Nemesis would be the perfect Imaginary Friends for their kids. So they decided to adopt the superhero and his archenemy.

"So once again, the day is saved. Right, sidekick?" said Bloo.

"Sidekick? I'm not your sidekick. You're *my* sidekick!" Mac protested.

Bloo made a face. "You wish!"

I can't get enough of me either.

FOSTER'S HOME FOR IMAGINARY FRIENDS THE COMPLETE 1ST SEASON DVD

REMOTE CONTROL BLOOREGARD Q. KAZOO BY MATTEL®

Check it. Now there are 2 totally amazing ways to get more of me. There's a DVD with all the episodes and special features from my first year at Madame Foster's. And some cool Cartoon Network toys—including a remote-controlled, talking version of yours truly!

THEY'RE BOTH IN STORES NOW. HOW AWESOME IS THAT?

FOUR PUNCH-OUT EASTER EGG STANDS INSIDE

IMAGINARY FRIENDS ARE FOREVER!

When Mac teams up with Imaginary Man, an awesome-rific superhero, his best friend Blooregard Q. Kazoo turns super, too — superjealous, that is. So Blooregard secretly joins forces with Imaginary Man's girly archenemy, Nemesis, and becomes Lord Uniscorn, the greatest villain the world has ever known!

But when Nemesis and Lord Uniscorn lay a trap for Imaginary Man, Uniscorn's true identity is revealed! Will he lose his best friend — forever?

ISBN-13: 978-0-439-899
ISBN-10: 0-439-89949-4
EAN
9 780439 899499

SCHOLASTIC

www.scholastic.com

CARTOON NETWORK